THE STRENGTH OF MEN

BY

JAMES OLIVER CURWOOD

British Library Cataloguing-in-Publication Data
A catalogue record for this book is available from the
British Library

James Oliver Curwood

James Oliver 'Jim' Curwood was an American action-adventure writer and conservationist. He was born on 12th June, 1878, in Owosso, Michigan, USA – as the youngest of four children.

He left high school before graduation, but passed the entrance exam to the University of Michigan, where he enrolled in the English department and studied journalism. After two years, he quit college to become a reporter. In 1900, Curwood sold his first story while working for the Detroit News-Tribune, and after this, his career in writing was made. By 1909 he had saved enough money to travel to the Canadian northwest, a trip that provided the inspiration for his wilderness adventure stories. The success of his novels afforded him the opportunity to return to the Yukon and Alaska for several months each year – allowing Curwood to write more than thirty such books.

By 1922, Curwood's writings had made him a very wealthy man and he fulfilled a childhood fantasy by building 'Curwood Castle' in Owosso. Constructed in the style of an eighteenth century French Chateau, the estate overlooked the Shiawassee River, and made for a truly picturesque setting. In one of the homes' two large turrets, Curwood set up his writing studio. He also owned a camp in a remote area in Baraga County, Michigan, near the Huron Mountains as well as a cabin in Roscommon, Michigan.

Curwood's adventure writing followed in the tradition of Jack London. Like London, Curwood set many of his works in the wilds of the Great Northwest and often used animals as lead characters (Kazan, Baree; Son of Kazan, The Grizzly King and Nomads of the North). Many of Curwood's adventure novels also feature romance as primary or secondary plot consideration. This approach gave his work broad commercial appeal and helped drive his appearance on several best-seller lists in the early 1920s. His most successful work was his 1920 novel, The River's End. The book sold more than 100,000 copies and was the fourth best-selling title of the year in the United States, according to Publisher's Weekly. He contributed to various literary and popular magazines throughout his career, and his bibliography includes more than 200 such articles, short stories and serializations.

Curwood was an avid hunter in his youth; however, as he grew older, he became an advocate of environmentalism and was appointed to the 'Michigan Conservation Commission' in 1926. The change in his attitude toward wildlife can be best expressed by a quote he gave in The Grizzly King: that 'The greatest thrill is not to kill but to let live.' Despite this change in attitude, Curwood did not have an ultimately fruitful relationship with nature. In 1927, while on a fishing trip in Florida, Curwood was bitten on the thigh by what was believed to have been a spider and he had an immediate allergic reaction. Health problems related to the bite escalated over the next few months as an infection set in. He died soon after in his nearby home on Williams Street, on 13th August 1927. He was aged just forty-nine, and was interred in Oak Hill Cemetery (Owosso), in a family plot.

Curwood's legacy lives on however, and his home of Curwood Castle is now a museum. During the first full weekend in June of each year, the city of Owosso holds the Curwood Festival to celebrate the city's heritage, and in addition, a mountain in L'Anse Township, Michigan was given the name Mount Curwood, and the L'Anse Township Park was renamed Curwood Park.

THE STRENGTH OF MEN

There was the scent of battle in the air. The whole of Porcupine City knew that it was coming, and every man and woman in its two hundred population held their breath in anticipation of the struggle between two men for a fortune—and a girl. For in some mysterious manner rumor of the girl had got abroad, passing from lip to lip, until even the children knew that there was some other thing than gold that would play a part in the fight between Clarry O'Grady and Jan Larose. On the surface it was not scheduled to be a fight with fists or guns. But in Porcupine City there were a few who knew the "inner story"—the story of the girl, as well as the gold, and those among them who feared the law would have arbitrated in a different manner for the two men if it had been in their power. But law is law, and the code was the code. There was no alternative. It was an unusual situation, and yet apparently simple of solution. Eighty miles north, as the canoe was driven, young Jan Larose had one day staked out a rich "find" at the headwaters of Pelican Creek. The same day, but later, Clarry O'Grady had driven his stakes beside Jan's. It had been a race to the mining recorder's office, and they had come in neck and neck. Popular sentiment favored Larose, the slim, quiet, dark-eyed half Frenchman. But there was the law, which had no sentiment. The recorder had sent an agent north to investigate. If there were two sets of stakes there could be but one verdict. Both claims would be thrown out, and then—

All knew what would happen, or thought that they knew. It would be a magnificent race to see who could set out fresh stakes and return to the recorder's office ahead of the other. It would be a fight of brawn and brain, unless—and those few who knew the "inner story" spoke softly among themselves.

An ox in strength, gigantic in build, with a face that for days had worn a sneering smile of triumph, O'Grady was already picked as a ten-to-one winner. He was a magnificent canoeman, no man in Porcupine City could equal him for endurance, and for his bow paddle he had the best Indian in the whole Reindeer Lake country. He stalked up and down the one street of Porcupine City, treating to drinks, cracking rough jokes, and offering wagers, while Jan Larose and his long-armed Cree sat quietly in the shade of the recorder's office waiting for the final moment to come.

There were a few of those who knew the "inner story" who saw something besides resignation and despair in Jan's quiet aloofness, and in the disconsolate droop of his head. His face turned a shade whiter when O'Grady passed near, dropping insult and taunt, and looking sidewise at him in a way that only HE could understand. But he made no retort, though his dark eyes glowed with a fire that never quite died—unless it was when, alone and unobserved, he took from his pocket a bit of buckskin in which was a silken tress of curling brown hair. Then his eyes shone with a light that was soft and luminous, and one seeing him then would have known that it was not a dream of gold that filled his heart, but of a brown-haired girl who had broken it.

On this day, the forenoon of the sixth since the agent had departed into the north, the end of the tense period of waiting was expected. Porcupine City had almost ceased to carry on the daily monotony of business. A score were lounging about the recorder's office. Women looked forth at frequent intervals through the open doors of the "city's" cabins, or gathered in two and threes to discuss this biggest sporting event ever known in the history of the town. Not a minute but scores of anxious eyes were turned searchingly up the river, down which the returning agent's canoe would first appear. With the dawn of this day O'Grady had refused to drink. He was stripped to the waist. His laugh was louder. Hatred as well as triumph glittered in his eyes, for to-day Jan Larose looked him coolly and squarely in the face, and nodded whenever he passed. It was almost noon when Jan spoke a few low words to his watchful Indian and walked to the top of the cedar-capped ridge that sheltered Porcupine City from the north winds.

From this ridge he could look straight into the north— the north where he was born. Only the Cree knew that for five nights he had slept, or sat awake, on the top of this ridge, with his face turned toward the polar star, and his heart breaking with loneliness and grief. Up there, far beyond where the green-topped forests and the sky seemed to meet, he could see a little cabin nestling under the stars—and Marie. Always his mind traveled back to the beginning of things, no matter how hard he tried to forget—even to the old days of years and years ago when he had toted the little Marie around on his back, and had crumpled her brown curls, and had revealed to her one by one the marvelous mysteries of the wilderness, with never a thought of the wonderful love that was to come. A half frozen little outcast brought in from the deep snows one day by Marie's father, he became first her playmate and brother—and after that lived in a few swift years of paradise and dreams. For Marie he had made of himself what he was. He had gone to Montreal. He had learned to read and write, he worked for the Company, he came to know the outside world, and at last the Government employed him. This was a triumph. He could still see the glow of pride and love in Marie's beautiful eyes when he came home after those two years in the great city. The Government sent for him each autumn after that. Deep into the wilderness he led the men who made the red and black lined maps. It was he who blazed out the northern limit of Banksian pine, and his name was in Government reports down in black and white—so that Marie and all the world could read.

One day he came back—and he found Clarry O'Grady at the Cummins' cabin. He had been there for a month with a broken leg. Perhaps it was the dangerous knowledge of the power of her beauty—the woman's instinct in her to tease with her prettiness, that led to Marie's flirtation with O'Grady. But Jan could not understand, and she played with fire—the fire of two hearts instead of one. The world went to pieces under Jan after that. There came the day when, in fair fight, he choked the taunting sneer from O'Grady's face back in the woods. He fought like a tiger, a mad demon. No one ever knew of that fight. And with the demon still raging in his breast he faced the girl. He could never quite remember what he had said. But it was terrible—and came straight from his soul. Then he went out, leaving Marie standing there white and silent. He did not go back. He had sworn never to do that, and during the weeks that followed it spread about that Marie Cummins had turned down Jan Larose, and that Clarry O'Grady was now the lucky man. It was one of the unexplained tricks of fate that had brought them together, and had set their discovery stakes side by side on Pelican Creek.

To-day, in spite of his smiling coolness, Jan's heart rankled with a bitterness that seemed to be concentrated of all the dregs that had ever entered into his life. It poisoned

him, heart and soul. He was not a coward. He was not afraid
of O'Grady.

And yet he knew that fate had already played the cards
against him. He would lose. He was almost confident of
that, even while he nerved himself to fight. There was the
drop of savage superstition in him, and he told himself that
something would happen to beat him out. O'Grady had
gone into the home that was almost his own and had robbed
him of Marie. In that fight in the forest he should have killed
him. That would have been justice, as he knew it. But he had
relented, half for Marie's sake, and half because he hated to
take a human life, even though it were O'Grady's. But this
time there would be no relenting. He had come alone to
the top of the ridge to settle the last doubts with himself.
Whoever won out, there would be a fight. It would be a
magnificent fight, like that which his grandfather had fought
and won for the honor of a woman years and years ago. He
was even glad that O'Grady was trying to rob him of what
he had searched for and found. There would be twice the
justice in killing him now. And it would be done fairly, as his
grandfather had done it.

Suddenly there came a piercing shout from the direction
of the river, followed by a wild call for him through Jackpine's
moose-horn. He answered the Cree's signal with a yell and
tore down through the bush. When he reached the foot of
the ridge at the edge of the clearing he saw the men, women

and children of Porcupine City running to the river. In front of the recorder's office stood Jackpine, bellowing through his horn. O'Grady and his Indian were already shoving their canoe out into the stream, and even as he looked there came a break in the line of excited spectators, and through it hurried the agent toward the recorder's cabin.

Side by side, Jan and his Indian ran to their canoe. Jackpine was stripped to the waist, like O'Grady and his Chippewayan. Jan threw off only his caribou-skin coat. His dark woolen shirt was sleeveless, and his long slim arms, as hard as ribbed steel, were free. Half the crowd followed him. He smiled, and waved his hand, the dark pupils of his eyes shining big and black. Their canoe shot out until it was within a dozen yards of the other, and those ashore saw him laugh into O'Grady's sullen, set face. He was cool. Between smiling lips his white teeth gleamed, and the women stared with brighter eyes and flushed cheeks, wondering how Marie Cummins could have given up this man for the giant hulk and drink-reddened face of his rival. Those among the men who had wagered heavily against him felt a misgiving. There was something in Jan's smile that was more than coolness, and it was not bravado. Even as he smiled ashore, and spoke in low Cree to Jackpine, he felt at the belt that he had hidden under the caribou-skin coat. There were two sheaths there, and two knives, exactly alike. It was thus that his grandfather had set forth one summer day to avenge a wrong, nearly seventy years before.

The agent had entered the cabin, and now he reappeared, wiping his sweating face with a big red handkerchief. The recorder followed. He paused at the edge of the stream and made a megaphone of his hands.

"Gentlemen," he cried raucously, "both claims have been thrown out!"

A wild yell came from O'Grady. In a single flash four paddles struck the water, and the two canoes shot bow and bow up the stream toward the lake above the bend. The crowd ran even with them until the low swamp at the lake's edge stopped them. In that distance neither had gained a yard advantage. But there was a curious change of sentiment among those who returned to Porcupine City. That night betting was no longer two and three to one on O'Grady. It was even money.

For the last thing that the men of Porcupine City had seen was that cold, quiet smile of Jan Larose, the gleam of his teeth, the something in his eyes that is more to be feared among men than bluster and brute strength. They laid it to confidence. None guessed that this race held for Jan no thought of the gold at the end. None guessed that he was following out the working of a code as old as the name of his race in the north.

As the canoes entered the lake the smile left Jan's face. His lips tightened until they were almost a straight line. His eyes grew darker, his breath came more quickly. For a little while O'Grady's canoe drew steadily ahead of them, and when Jackpine's strokes went deeper and more powerful Jan spoke to him in Cree, and guided the canoe so that it cut straight as an arrow in O'Grady's wake. There was an advantage in that. It was small, but Jan counted on the cumulative results of good generalship.

His eyes never for an instant left O'Grady's huge, naked back. Between his knees lay his .303 rifle. He had figured on the fraction of time it would take him to drop his paddle, pick up the gun, and fire. This was his second point in generalship—getting the drop on O'Grady.

Once or twice in the first half hour O'Grady glanced back over his shoulder, and it was Jan who now laughed tauntingly at the other. There was something in that laugh that sent a chill through O'Grady. It was as hard as steel, a sort of madman's laugh.

It was seven miles to the first portage, and there were nine in the eighty-mile stretch. O'Grady and his Chippewayan were a hundred yards ahead when the prow of their canoe touched shore. They were a hundred and fifty ahead when both canoes were once more in the water on the other side of the portage, and O'Grady sent back a hoarse shout of triumph. Jan hunched himself a little lower. He spoke to

Jackpine—and the race began. Swifter and swifter the canoes cut through the water. From five miles an hour to six, from six to six and a half—seven—seven and a quarter, and then the strain told. A paddle snapped in O'Grady's hands with a sound like a pistol shot. A dozen seconds were lost while he snatched up a new paddle and caught the Chippewayan's stroke, and Jan swung close into their wake again. At the end of the fifteenth mile, where the second portage began, O'Grady was two hundred yards in the lead. He gained another twenty on the portage and with a breath that was coming now in sobbing swiftness Jan put every ounce of strength behind the thrust of his paddle. Slowly they gained. Foot by foot, yard by yard, until for a third time they cut into O'Grady's wake. A dull pain crept into Jan's back. He felt it slowly creeping into his shoulders and to his arms. He looked at Jackpine and saw that he was swinging his body more and more with the motion of his arms. And then he saw that the terrific pace set by O'Grady was beginning to tell on the occupants of the canoe ahead. The speed grew less and less, until it was no more than seventy yards. In spite of the pains that were eating at his strength like swimmer's cramp, Jan could not restrain a low cry of exultation. O'Grady had planned to beat him out in that first twenty-mile spurt. And he had failed! His heart leaped with new hope even while his strokes were growing weaker.

Ahead of them, at the far end of the lake, there loomed up the black spruce timber which marked the beginning of the third portage, thirty miles from Porcupine City. Jan knew that he would win there—that he would gain an eighth of a mile in the half-mile carry. He knew of a shorter cut than that of the regular trail. He had cleared it himself, for he had spent a whole winter on that portage trapping lynx.

Marie lived only twelve miles beyond. More than once Marie had gone with him over the old trap line. She had helped him to plan the little log cabin he had built for himself on the edge of the big swamp, hidden away from all but themselves. It was she who had put the red paper curtains over the windows, and who, one day, had written on the corner of one of them: "My beloved Jan." He forgot O'Grady as he thought of Marie and those old days of happiness and hope. It was Jackpine who recalled him at last to what was happening. In amazement he saw that O'Grady and his Chippewayan had ceased paddling. They passed a dozen yards abreast of them. O'Grady's great arms and shoulders were glistening with perspiration. His face was purplish. In his eyes and on his lips was the old taunting sneer. He was panting like a wind-broken animal. As Jan passed he uttered no word.

An eighth of a mile ahead was the point where the regular portage began, but Jan swung around this into a shallow inlet from which his own secret trail was cut. Not until he was ashore did he look back. O'Grady and his Indian were paddling in a leisurely manner toward the head of the point. For a moment it looked as though they had given up the race, and Jan's heart leaped exultantly. O'Grady saw him and waved his hand. Then he jumped out to his knees in the water and the Chippewayan followed him. He shouted to Jan, and pointed down at the canoe. The next instant, with a powerful shove, he sent the empty birchbark speeding far out into the open water.

Jan caught his breath. He heard Jackpine's cry of amazement behind him. Then he saw the two men start on a swift run over the portage trail, and with a fierce, terrible cry he sprang toward his rifle, which he had leaned against a tree.

In that moment he would have fired, but O'Grady and the Indian had disappeared into the timber. He understood— O'Grady had tricked him, as he had tricked him in other ways. He had a second canoe waiting for him at the end of the portage, and perhaps others farther on. It was unfair. He could still hear O'Grady's taunting laughter as it had rung out in Porcupine City, and the mystery of it was solved. His blood grew hot—so hot that his eyes burned, and his breath seemed to parch his lips. In that short space in which he stood paralyzed and unable to act his brain blazed like a volcano. Who—was helping O'Grady by having a canoe ready for him at the other side of the portage? He knew that no man had gone North from Porcupine City during those tense days of waiting. The code which all understood had prohibited that. Who, then, could it be?—who but Marie herself! In some way O'Grady had got word to her, and it was the Cummins' canoe that was waiting for him!

With a strange cry Jan lifted the bow of the canoe to his shoulder and led Jackpine in a run. His strength had returned. He did not feel the whiplike sting of boughs that struck him across the face. He scarcely looked at the little cabin of logs when they passed it. Deep down in his heart he called upon the Virgin to curse those two—Marie Cummins and Clarry O'Grady, the man and the girl who had cheated him out of love, out of home, out of everything he had possessed, and who were beating him now through perfidy and trickery.

His face and his hands were scratched and bleeding when they came to the narrow waterway, half lake and half river, which let into the Blind Loon. Another minute and they were racing again through the water. From the mouth of the channel he saw O'Grady and the Chippewayan a quarter of a mile ahead. Five miles beyond them was the fourth portage. It was hidden now by a thick pall of smoke rising slowly into the clear sky. Neither Jan nor the Indian had caught the pungent odors of burning forests in the air, and they knew that it was a fresh fire. Never in the years that Jan could remember had that portage been afire, and he wondered if this was another trick of O'Grady's. The fire spread rapidly as they advanced. It burst forth in a dozen places along the shore of the lake, sending up huge volumes of black smoke riven by lurid tongues of flame. O'Grady and his canoe became less and less distinct. Finally they disappeared entirely in the lowering clouds of the conflagration. Jan's eyes searched the water as they approached shore, and at last he saw what he had expected to find—O'Grady's empty canoe drifting slowly away from the beach. O'Grady and the Chippewayan were gone.

Over that half-mile portage Jan staggered with his eyes half closed and his breath coming in gasps. The smoke blinded him, and at times the heat of the fire scorched his face. In several places it had crossed the trail, and the hot embers burned through their moccasins. Once Jackpine uttered a cry of pain. But Jan's lips were set. Then, above the roar of the flames sweeping down upon the right of them, he caught the low thunder of Dead Man's Whirlpool and the cataract that had made the portage necessary. From the heated earth their feet came to a narrow ledge of rock, worn smooth by the furred and moccasined tread of centuries, with the chasm on one side of them and a wall of rock on the other. Along the crest of that wall, a hundred feet above them, the fire swept in a tornado of flame and smoke. A tree crashed behind them, a dozen seconds too late. Then the trail widened and sloped down into the dip that ended the portage. For an instant Jan paused to get his bearing, and behind him Jackpine shouted a warning.

Up out of the smoldering oven where O'Grady should have found his canoe two men were rushing toward them. They were O'Grady and the Chippewayan. He caught the gleam of a knife in the Indian's hand. In O'Grady's there was something larger and darker—a club, and Jan dropped his end of the canoe with a glad cry, and drew one of the knives from his belt. Jackpine came to his side, with his hunting knife in his hand, measuring with glittering eyes the oncoming foe of his race—the Chippewayan.

And Jan laughed softly to himself, and his teeth gleamed again, for at last fate was playing his game. The fire had burned O'Grady's canoe, and it was to rob him of his own canoe that O'Grady was coming to fight. A canoe! He laughed again, while the fire roared over his head and the whirlpool thundered at his feet. O'Grady would fight for a canoe—for gold—while he—HE—would fight for something else, for the vengeance of a man whose soul and honor had been sold. He cared nothing for the canoe. He cared nothing for the gold. He told himself, in this one tense moment of waiting, that he cared no longer for Marie. It was the fulfillment of the code.

He was still smiling when O'Grady was so near that he could see the red glare in his eyes. There was no word, no shout, no sound of fury or defiance as the two men stood for an instant just out of striking distance. Jan heard the coming together of Jackpine and the Chippewayan. He heard them straggling, but not the flicker of an eyelash did his gaze leave O'Grady's face. Both men understood. This time had to come. Both had expected it, even from that day of the fight in the woods when fortune had favored Jan. The burned canoe had only hastened the hour a little. Suddenly Jan's free hand reached behind him to his belt. He drew forth the second knife and tossed it at O'Grady's feet.

O'Grady made a movement to pick it up, and then, while Jan was partly off his guard, came at him with a powerful swing of the club. It was his catlike quickness, the quickness almost of the great northern loon that evades a rifle ball, that had won for Jan in the forest fight. It saved him now. The club cut through the air over his head, and, carried by the momentum of his own blow, O'Grady lurched against him with the full force of his two hundred pounds of muscle and bone. Jan's knife swept in an upward flash and plunged to the hilt through the flesh of his enemy's forearm. With a cry of pain O'Grady dropped his club, and the two crashed to the stone floor of the trail. This was the attack that Jan had feared and tried to foil, and with a lightning-like squirming movement he swung himself half free, and on his back, with O'Grady's huge hands linking at his throat, he drew back his knife arm for the fatal plunge.

In this instant, so quick that he could scarcely have taken a breath in the time, his eyes took in the other struggle between Jackpine and the Chippewayan. The two Indians had locked themselves in a deadly embrace. All thought of masters, of life or death, were forgotten in the roused-up hatred that fired them now in their desire to kill. They had drawn close to the edge of the chasm. Under them the thundering roar of the whirlpool was unheard, their ears caught no sound of the moaning surge of the flames far over their heads. Even as Jan stared horror-stricken in that one moment, they locked at the edge of the chasm. Above the tumult of the flood below and the fire above there rose a wild yell, and the two plunged down into the abyss, locked and fighting even as they fell in a twisting, formless shape to the death below.

It happened in an instant—like the flash of a quick picture on a screen—and even as Jan caught the last of Jackpine's terrible face, his hand drove eight inches of steel toward O'Grady's body. The blade struck something hard—something that was neither bone nor flesh, and he drew back again to strike. He had struck the steel buckle on O'Grady's belt. This time—

A sudden hissing roar filled the air. Jan knew that he did not strike—but he scarcely knew more than that in the first shock of the fiery avalanche that had dropped upon them from the rock wall of the mountain. He was conscious of fighting desperately to drag himself from under a weight that was not O'Grady's—a weight that stifled the breath in his lungs, that crackled in his ears, that scorched his face and his hands, and was burning out his eyes. A shriek rang in his ears unlike any other cry of man he had ever heard, and he knew that it was O'Grady's. He pulled himself out, foot by foot, until fresher air struck his nostrils, and dragged himself nearer and nearer to the edge of the chasm. He could not rise. His limbs were paralyzed. His knife arm dragged at his side. He opened his eyes and found that he could see. Where they had fought was the smoldering ruin of a great tree, and standing out of the ruin of that tree, half naked, his hands tearing wildly at his face, was O'Grady. Jan's fingers clutched at a small rock. He called out, but there was no meaning to the sound he made. Clarry O'Grady threw out his great arms.

"Jan—Jan Larose—" he cried. "My God, don't strike now! I'm blind—blind—"

He staggered back, as if expecting a blow. "Don't strike!" he almost shrieked. "Mother of Heaven—my eyes are burned out—I'm blind—blind—"

He backed to the wall, his huge form crouched, his hands reaching out as if to ward off the deathblow. Jan tried to move, and the effort brought a groan of agony to his lips. A second crash filled his ears as a second avalanche of fiery debris plunged down upon the trail farther back. He stared straight up through the stifling smoke. Lurid tongues of flame were leaping over the wall of the mountain where the edge of the forest was enveloped in a sea of twisting and seething fire. It was only a matter of minutes—perhaps seconds. Death had them both in its grip.

He looked again at O'Grady, and there was no longer the desire for the other's life in his heart. He could see that the giant was unharmed, except for his eyes.

"Listen, O'Grady," he cried. "My legs are broken, I guess, and I can't move. It's sure death to stay here another minute. You can get away. Follow the wall—to your right. The slope is still free of fire, and—and—"

O'Grady began to move, guiding himself slowly along the wall. Then, suddenly, he stopped.

"Jan Larose—you say you can't move?" he shouted.

"Yes."

Slowly O'Grady turned and came gropingly toward the sound of Jan's voice. Jan held tight to the rock that he had gripped in his left hand. Was it possible that O'Grady would kill him now, stricken as he was? He tried to drag himself to a new position, but his effort was futile.

"Jan! Jan Larose!" called O'Grady, stopping to listen.

Jan held his breath. Then the truth seemed to dawn upon O'Grady. He laughed, differently than he had laughed before, and stretched out his arms.

"My God, Jan," he cried, "you don't think I'm clean BEAST, do you? The fight's over, man, an' I guess God A'mighty brought this on us to show what fools we was. Where are y', Jan Larose? I'm goin' t' carry you out!"

"I'm here!" called Jan.

He could see truth and fearlessness in O'Grady's sightless face, and he guided him without fear. Their hands met. Then O'Grady lowered himself and hoisted Jan to his shoulders as easily as he would have lifted a boy. He straightened himself and drew a deep breath, broken by a stabbing throb of pain.

"I'm blind an' I won't see any more," he said, "an' mebbe you won't ever walk any more. But if we ever git to that gold I kin do the work and you kin show me how. Now—p'int out the way, Jan Larose!"

With his arms clasped about O'Grady's naked shoulders, Jan's smarting eyes searched through the thickening smother of fire and smoke for a road that the other's feet might tread. He shouted "Left"—"right"—"right"—"right"—"left" into this blind companion's ears until they touched the wall. As the heat smote them more fiercely, O'Grady bowed his great head upon his chest and obeyed mutely the signals that rang in his ears. The bottoms of his moccasins were burned from his feet, live embers ate at his flesh, his broad chest was a fiery blister, and yet he strode on straight into the face of still greater heat and greater torture, uttering no sound that could be heard above the steady roar of the flames. And Jan, limp and helpless on his back, felt then the throb and pulse of a giant life under him, the straining of thick neck, of massive shoulders and the grip of powerful arms whose strength told him that at last he had found the comrade and the man in Clarry O'Grady. "Right"—"left"—"left"—"right" he shouted, and then he called for O'Grady to stop in a voice that was shrill with warning.

"There's fire ahead," he yelled. "We can't follow the wall any longer. There's an open space close to the chasm. We can make that, but there's only about a yard to spare. Take short steps—one step each time I tell you. Now—left—left—left—left—"

Like a soldier on drill, O'Grady kept time with his scorched feet until Jan turned him again to face the storm of fire, while one of his own broken legs dangled over the abyss into which Jackpine and the Chippewayan had plunged to their death. Behind them, almost where they had fought, there crashed down a third avalanche from the edge of the mountain. Not a shiver ran through O'Grady's great body. Steadily and unflinchingly—step—step—step—he went ahead, while the last threads of his moccasins smoked and burned. Jan could no longer see half a dozen yards in advance. A wall of black smoke rose in their faces, and he pulled O'Grady's ear:

"We've got just one chance, Clarry. I can't see any more. Keep straight ahead—and run for it, and may the good God help us now!"

And Clarry O'Grady, drawing one great breath that was half fire into his lungs, ran straight into the face of what looked like death to Jan Larose. In that one moment Jan closed his eyes and waited for the plunge over the cliff. But in place of death a sweep of air that seemed almost cold struck his face, and he opened his eyes to find the clear and uncharred slope leading before them down to the edge of the lake. He shouted the news into O'Grady's ear, and then there arose from O'Grady's chest a great sobbing cry, partly of joy, partly of pain, and more than all else of that terrible grief which came of the knowledge that back in the pit of death from which he had escaped he had left forever the vision of life itself. He dropped Jan in the edge of the water, and, plunging in to his waist, he threw handful after handful of water into his own swollen face, and then stared upward, as though this last experiment was also his last hope.

"My God, I'm blind—stone blind!"

Jan was staring hard into O'Grady's face. He called him nearer, took the swollen and blackened face between his two hands, and his voice was trembling with joy when he spoke.

"You're not blind—not for good—O'Grady," he said. "I've seen men like you before—twice. You—you'll get well.

O'Grady—Clarry O'Grady—let's shake! I'm a brother to
you from this day on. And I'm glad—glad—that Marie loves
a man like you!"

O'Grady had gripped his hand, but he dropped it now
as though it had been one of the live brands that had hurtled
down upon them from the top of the mountain.

"Marie—man—why—she HATES me!" he cried. "It's
you—YOU—Jan Larose, that she loves! I went there with
a broken leg, an' I fell in love with her. But she wouldn't
so much as let me touch her hand, an' she talked of you—
always—always—until I had learned to hate you before you
came. I dunno why she did it—that other thing—unless
it was to make you jealous. I guess it was all f'r fun, Jan.
She didn't know. The day you went away she sent me after
you. But I hated you—hated you worse'n she hated me. It's
you—you—"

He clutched his hands at his sightless face again, and
suddenly Jan gave a wild shout. Creeping around the edge
of a smoking headland, he had caught sight of a man and a
canoe.

"There's a man in a canoe!" he cried, "He sees us!
O'Grady—"

He tried to lift himself, but fell back with a groan. Then
he laughed, and, in spite of his agony, there was a quivering
happiness in his voice.

"He's coming, O'Grady. And it looks—it looks like a canoe we both know. We'll go back to her cabin together, O'Grady. And when we're on our legs again—well, I never wanted the gold. That's yours—all of it."

A determined look had settled in O'Grady's face. He groped his way to Jan's side, and their hands met in a clasp that told more than either could have expressed of the brotherhood and strength of men.

"You can't throw me off like that, Jan Larose," he said. "We're pardners!"